Blood & Poison

Richard Foreman

Copyright © Richard Foreman 2023.

The right of Richard Foreman to be identified as the author of this work has been asserted by him in accordance with the Copyright, Designs and Patents Act, 1988.

First published as a novella in 2023 by Sharpe Books.

SPIES OF ROME: BLOOD & POISON

Friends in High Places

Even more than in a brothel, Rufus Varro felt at home in a tavern. The smell of second-rate wine in his nostrils was better than the sound of music in his ears. It was a busy, bustling evening. Plenty of Romans were trying to find answers, or better still oblivion, at the bottom of a wine jug.

The landlord, Fabius Bulla, grinned and rubbed his hands together more than once, anticipating healthy takings for the night. He would aim to keep the good news from his wife, lest she spend the money on a garish bauble or new stola. Instead, Bulla intended to devote the extra coin to his mistress, Marcella. There were several new faces dotted around the place. Even Hannibal Barca or his mother-in-law would be welcome, however, if they spent sufficient money - Bulla thought to himself. The landlord flirted with the idea of buying Marcella some perfume. It would be cheap perfume, but she would show her appreciation, nonetheless.

It was not the first time that Varro, a wastrel turned spy, had frequented *The Silver Cup* (there were few establishments in the Subura that the poet and once dissolute youth was unfamiliar with) but he was not a regular. A handful of patrons eyed Varro with a little suspicion, or envy. The handsome stranger, whose expression fluctuated between shades of amusement and anxiety, wore a tunic which was too finely woven for their liking. The dagger hanging down from his belt betrayed a certain wealth and rank too.

Varro surveyed the scene as he took another mouthful of wine. Initially, the spy glanced at the exits, to check that they remained unblocked. There was always the chance that he would need to make a hasty, strategic retreat. Varro wryly smiled as he observed a bedraggled patron in the corner. He had recently been burying his head in his wide-brimmed cup. He was now burying his head in the bosom of a buxom whore. He groaned a little, while she tenderly stroked his thinning hair as if he were a child. No doubt she would wake him up, Varro thought, when she needed the drunk to make a second payment. The sound of a slap, followed by cackle, whip-cracked in the air as a flat-faced docker struck the rump of a serving girl. The initial displeasure on her expression soon transformed into delight when she turned to the customer and offered up a gap-toothed smile, in the hope of improving her tip.

The main door creaked open once more and Varro turned to see if it was Dio. But it was just another bearded, bleary-eyed stranger. Dio was late. But he had often been tardy, the spy recalled, during nights spent drinking and whoring all those years ago. Varro tapped his foot, in anxiety or impatience, yet the quilt of sawdust on the warped floorboards softened the sound.

He cursed Dio, beneath his breath, for keeping him waiting. Varro also cursed Marcus Agrippa, for sending him on the potential deadly mission.

Varro had attended a party last month, to celebrate either a friend's marriage or divorce, at which Agrippa had been present. Caesar's lieutenant cornered his agent in the garden, just as Varro was intending to stalk the prey of the host's daughter. They exchanged pleasantries, beside a worn and chipped marble statue of Diana. The piece had seen better days, Varro fancied. Agrippa asked after Manius, his bodyguard. Manius was away from Rome, taking his wife, Camilla, to the coast. Varro feigned interest in Agrippa's latest building project and asked after his wife, Claudia. The Second Man of Rome pursed his lips and rolled his eyes, before replying:

"She sees more of her latest astrologer than me nowadays, thankfully. I try to keep out of her way – and she keeps out of mine. I warrant that there are more unhappier marriages in Rome."

In hindsight, Varro realised that the wily statesman strategically then steered the conversation towards the subject of his agent's time as a young poet – and the company he kept as an adolescent.

"You were friends with Marcus Sosius and Publius Dio, were you not?" Agrippa asked, almost innocently. Almost.

"Yes, not that I can recall much about that period now. If you drink a sufficient surplus of wine, it is tantamount to drinking from the waters of Lethe."

"Yet you were a trusted companion of Dio?"

"We shared the odd jug of Calenum, and also the odd mistress."

"Do you still correspond with him?"

"No, why do you ask?" Varro remarked. The spy's suspicions were duly aroused. But it was too late.

Agrippa creased his brow, in either condemnation or worry, before he answered:

"Publius Dio is an enemy of the state. He has made a career of procuring rare and valuable items for various wealthy clients. Initially, he procured women - and young girls and boys - for the elite in Rome, with particular or peculiar tastes. His services also include arranging exotic beasts, to feed the appetite for our games – or the creatures are used as prey, for those who can afford to hunt. Silks, rare spices and precious gems – Dio can provide them all, for a price. His criminal activities also extend to bribery and blackmail. More than one government official has been compromised or corrupted by Dio. The roots of his poisonous tree run deep and wide. The criminal or businessman, depending on how you view Dio, trades in information and intelligence. He is not averse to selling secrets to the enemies of the Caesar. I have recently been informed that Dio will soon be visiting Rome once more. He has in his possession a consignment of the poison, Nightshade. Nightshade is tasteless, odourless and deadly. The enemies of Rome could wipe out the imperial family during one meal together. A few doses of Nightshade could plunge us into another civil war. I am keen to apprehend both the seller and his goods. I will duly loosen the pernicious rogue's tongue, so he discloses the names of any confederates too."

"It seems that Publius became quite industrious and enterprising over the years. Whilst I toiled tirelessly at remaining a wastrel," Varro remarked, drily, as he glanced over Agrippa's shoulder again. He was trying to discern whether the host's daughter, like the statue of Diana, had seen better days.

"As much as Dio has made a name for himself, however, he has proved successful in maintaining his anonymity. I once employed another agent to draw Dio out, but he is cautious and clever. He is well-connected and possesses friends in high places. The fox employs proxies and impostors to carry out his business dealings. Few people are even aware of his appearance. He could be at this party, and I would not recognise the cur. But you would, Rufus. He may even approach you, being an old friend and drinking companion. Your mission, when, rather than if, you decide to accept it, is to arrange a meeting with Dio. Reach out to mutual acquaintances and convey how keen you are to see him again. I can provide you with some names too, who I believe are trusted clients. You can bait the hook by expressing an interest in a business opportunity. If he does not reach out to you as an old friend, he might as a new customer."

Varro reached out to his old friend through third parties and - unfortunately - Dio contacted him in return to arrange a meeting. The reluctant spy reported his success to Agrippa. "I want Dio to feel comfortable, that he is in control. Allow him to choose the venue and timing of any meet. I will still scoop him up, like a fish in a net."

Agrippa had called the fixer "a rumour, as much as a man" but Varro knew Dio to be all too real. The stories about him were also doubtless true - unfortunately. Dio employed a small army of gladiators and former soldiers to serve as enforcers and bodyguards. They were not averse to breaking bones and torching properties. If the price was right, Dio would also hire his personnel out as assassins. He had been known to employ a surgeon in his retinue as well. A client had once refused to pay for services provided. Dio instructed the surgeon to amputate his left arm, mindful that he still wanted the payee alive, so he could redeem any monies owed. Varro recalled how his friend possessed a cruel streak, beneath a veneer of charm, even in his youth. The agent rightly feared earning Dio's wrath, but he judged that it might be preferable to earning the disappointment and displeasure of Agrippa – and the Emperor.

Publius Dio entered the tavern, wrinkling his nose a little at the unpleasant aromas and underwhelming décor. But it was a suitable enough venue to conduct business. Indeed, there wasn't a venue considered unsuitable in relation to conducting business, in Dio's eyes. A few grey streaks marked his shiny black hair, styled in a Pompey-like quiff. But otherwise, little had changed, concerning Dio's appearance, Varro fancied. Same serpentine features (wide, thin mouth; pronounced cheek bones; narrow, sly eyes). Same cleft-chin. Same confident, or arrogant, manner. Success had doubtless gifted the advocate's son an even greater sense of superiority, Varro thought. Dio had also retained his habit of wearing an ostentatious broach, to secure the finely woven cloak covering his tunic. The criminal appeared a paragon of respectability.

Dio was flanked by a couple of less respectable looking figures. Bodyguards. Former gladiators. Beneath their cloaks, Varro observed that they were carrying cudgels and daggers. Their broad faces were as gnarled and scarred as their knuckles. They appeared thoroughly unimpressed – and thoroughly intimidating. Varro imagined that the dogs might snarl or bark at any moment. He lamented the absence of Manius - and checked the exits once more. The agent was not completely useless in a fight, but he was far from confident about besting just one of Dio's bodyguards, let alone two of them.

"It has been a long time, Rufus. Too long. As much as we drowned ourselves in drink, I still remember some of the convivial times we had together. I cannot quite recall if you stole more women from me, or I from you, however," Dio remarked, opening his arms and then clasping Varro's hand in his, before sitting down. His mouth smiled, but the rest of his face refrained from doing so. "I dare say that we can agree that writing poetry was never going to make our fortunes. Tell me, how are you?"

"I'm still faithful to a belief of infidelity. I drink too much. Or not enough. Money slips through my fingers, like grains of sands. If I haven't contracted the pox already, I soon will. I have a senator's wife baying for my blood, even more than her husband is, and my debts are rising like the tide. In short, little has changed since I last saw you. But you are looking well and prospering, it seems."

"I make a good, dishonest living, you could say," Dio blithely remarked, before surveying the room once more. His eyes briefly darted about like a lizard's. "But let us get down to business, shall we? Time is money – and I do not like to needlessly waste either."

Varro explained his financial situation. His dire financial situation. He was close to ruin, he confessed. He had been foolish to marry, perhaps. But he had definitely been foolish to sign over one of his properties to his wife when they divorced. But ownership would revert to him, should his former wife, Lucilla, pass away. Varro seemingly let his wry, patrician mask slip and appeared desperate and ashamed (not least because he had to swallow his pride and ask an old friend to save him). He held his head in his hands, allowed his voice to break, chewed upon his lip and fidgeted with his wine cup. Agrippa had once mentioned to Varro that he was "a better actor than poet," which made him an effective agent. It wasn't that Varro wanted Dio to take pity on him. Rather, he wanted him to think that he could take advantage of the potential client across the table.

"I was told that you have the ways and means to help fix my problems. But I do not want Lucilla to suffer unduly. I would like things to be painless."

"That can be arranged. As you say, I have ways and means," Dio replied, eyeing Varro suspiciously. Or accusingly. His narrow eyes grew narrower. Cruel became crueller. He conceded that he would have been convinced by his old friend's performance, if he did not know that he was an agent of Marcus Agrippa. "Unfortunately for you, Rufus, I am not without ways and means in other areas. I am well aware of who your paymaster is - and why you invited me here this evening. I could afford to walk into your trap, though. Curiosity got the better of me. I perhaps would have laughed if someone told me that Rufus Varro had found gainful employment. Imagine my surprise when

SPIES OF ROME: BLOOD & POISON

it transpired that you were an agent of Rome. And a successful one, I dare say. You even got blood on your hands, when dealing with Lucius Scaurus. He was always more of a peacock than a lion. As you may know, Rufus, I am not unaccustomed to getting blood on my hands. I have done things that would even make a young Pompey or Fulvia blush. I cannot abide disloyalty and treachery. And you have proved disloyal and treacherous. A fault has been committed. That fault, wrongdoing, must be punished. Or paid for. If you are not already in debt, as you have just divulged, then you are indebted to me. Given our past friendship, I will permit you to settle your debt in coin. Should you refuse, you will pay your debt through a blood price. I will not shed your blood, at first, but I still believe that Fronto remains in your service. I was always fond of the old man. But every debt must be paid."

Dio remained remarkably calm as he spoke. Cold. Businesslike. Ironically, he considered that he was being generous in relation to the terms of the agreement that was being proposed. He had killed others for less serious transgressions. Dio had one eye on the fact that Varro could prove a valuable source of intelligence in the future, given his proximity to the Second Man of Rome.

Varro remained calm too, or even amused - that his performance had all been in vain. His handsome features hardened though, like molten bronze solidifying, when Dio issued the threat to harm his estate manager.

"I cannot allow you to leave, Publius," the agent stated, his voice as hard as his features. Beneath the table Varro's knuckles whitened, as he clasped his hand around his dagger.

Both men half-smiled at one another. But their thoughts were far from congenial. The tension in the air tightened, like a noose around a condemned man's neck. Dio was accustomed to issuing orders and threats, rather than receiving them. For a brief, but real, moment he was tempted to instruct his bodyguards to slit the agent's throat – and wipe the half-smile off his face. Instead, Dio laughed – albeit slightly unpleasantly. It was the same laugh he emitted when victims of torture pleaded to be shown mercy.

"And who is going to prevent me? You and whose army?" Dio remarked, his usually smooth features now corrugated in a sneer.

"Caesar's," Marcus Agrippa posited, in a voice infused with duty and determination, as he got to his feet. The Second Man of Rome was wearing clothes fit for a dock worker. His face was dusted with dirt, his hat covered his glossy hair. A dozen other similarly disguised figures rose to their feet too. Soldiers. Ready to follow orders. Despite his rank, Agrippa was willing to be the first to draw his blade and bloody it. The general knew how to fight – and win.

Dio's eyes widened. His sneer grew even more pronounced. The criminal, survivor, businessman quickly assessed the situation. The odds were against him to fight his way out of the trap that had been set for him. But there would be no need to fight anyway. As much as anger fired his heart, his tone was playful when he spoke. He also raised his hand aloft, to signal to his bodyguards to stand down.

"Marcus Agrippa. I understand that you have met one of my proxies in the past. It's a pleasure to finally meet you."

"It may not feel like such a pleasure after I've finished with you, Publius," Agrippa replied. He would arrange to oversee the first interrogation himself.

"Perhaps we should have dinner after all this mistake has been rectified and this unpleasantness is over. This encounter comes a mild surprise, but I am not wholly unprepared for it. Life is a game – and I always endeavour to be one step ahead of my opponents. You may be considered a soldier. As such, allow me to present you with some orders," Dio politely said, forcing a smile and retrieving a scroll, which was tucked into the belt worn around his tunic."

His features sank, like so many vessels at the Battle of Actium. Not even Marcus Agrippa could be stoical about everything. He recognised the seal and handwriting, even before he scrutinised the contents. The spymaster had indeed been outplayed. The document provided its bearer with immunity. Dio had been endowed with Livia's "trust and authority". The Empress ordered that her agent should not be apprehended or prosecuted.

Augustus – and his wife – were laws unto themselves. Dio had friends in the highest of places. Alas, it was not uncommon in the world of intelligence for the left hand to not know what the right was doing. Agrippa suspected that the consignment of Nightshade was intended for the Empress. Used correctly, the imperial family could wipe out the enemies of Rome during just one meal together.

"I trust that you are satisfied?" Dio remarked, not without a shard of triumphalism. The agent was wary of wishing to bait the Second Man of Rome too much, however.

"I am not sure if satisfied is the word that I would quite use," Agrippa replied, handing the document back.

"My invitation to have dinner still stands. I look forward to doing business with you, not that we have been acquainted. We could do great things together," Dio cordially remarked, before turning to address his old friend. "It seems that, despite your newfound employment Rufus, you are still wasting your time. If we see each other again, I hope it will be in different circumstances - for your sake," the criminal said, with more than a hint of a warning.

Dio, along with his two dogs trailing behind him, departed. Varro appeared a little confounded. Agrippa appeared more than a little crestfallen. He didn't want to return home to an empty house, or one containing his wife.

"It seems that we have indeed wasted our time, Rufus. But let us not waste this wine," the Roman remarked, reaching for his purse, so he could pay for his men to get drunk too.

You cannot win every battle. Just make sure you win the war.

"What just happened?" Varro asked, whilst eyeing up a pretty serving girl over his paymaster's shoulder.

"Sometimes the bigger the fish you are, the easier it is to slip through the net."

RICHARD FOREMAN

A Night To Remember

Rufus Varro finally stirred. One of the shutters in his bedroom was open, letting in the breeze and an occasional insect. The sun seemed to throb in rhythm with his wine-soaked head. It was either late morning or early afternoon. Varro didn't much know or care. The sometime poet could afford to spend the day busy doing nothing, again.

He narrowed his eyes and tried to recall the events of yesternight at the party. It wasn't all a blur. Just some of it. He remembered the taste of the more than tolerable Setinum. He remembered talking to some old drinking companions, although their conversation was eminently forgettable. A senator introduced him to a business associate, who asked him to invest in a tin mine - whose returns were too good to be true. Varro remembered avoiding Lucretia, a former mistress - and her husband. He made a promise, which was as empty as his winecup at the time, to read over a fellow poet's latest verses. He remembered what the lissom, lustful woman looked like naked, after they disappeared upstairs to make use of their host's bedroom. He just couldn't, for the life of him, remember the woman's name.

The copious amount of wine the patrician had drunk over the years hadn't washed away Varro's fine features or ruined his figure. His expression, when untroubled or free from melancholy, was good-humoured. Varro knew how to laugh at life, drunk or sober. A fringe of curls concealed a scar on his forehead, from where the spy had been tortured during a mission to uncover a plot to overthrow the Emperor. It had been Varro's first mission. Unfortunately. it had not been his last. The erstwhile agent had recently been ordered by Marcus Agrippa to meet with Publius Dio, a drinking companion from his youth who was now a person of interest to the spymaster. The operation had not gone according to plan. The plan had been to apprehend Dio and confiscate a consignment of the deadly poison Nightshade. Yet the smuggler had somehow forged a business

SPIES OF ROME: BLOOD & POISON

relationship with the Empress, providing the criminal with immunity from prosecution in the courts.

Varro yawned, stretching out his tired body. He was content to go back to sleep.

"You have a visitor," Fronto remarked, standing at the door. The aged estate manager, who had also served under Varro's father, may have been frail of body - but his mind was still as sharp as a libertore's dagger. His face was creased in slight concern or slight disapproval.

"Can you not tell them I am unwell?"

"Marcus Agrippa didn't believe that excuse the first time. He is just as unlikely to believe it now," the dry-witted attendant replied.

Varro now sighed rather than yawned. There were not many men that he would rouse himself for and attend to immediately, but the Second Man of Rome - and spymaster - was one of them.

***

Marcus Agrippa was waiting, not a little impatiently, in the smartly furnished triclinium. The statesman still retained his soldierly build. He had been up since before dawn, working (overseeing architectural plans and budgets for building projects, digesting reports from governors and military commanders across the four corners of the empire, drafting coded communiques to agents in his extensive spy network). Agrippa was keen to fill each segment of his time, which is why he was less than impressed with Varro, who seemed happy to idle away entire days nursing a sore head in bed. Agrippa had been the right arm of Octavius (his sword-arm) since travelling with his friend to Rome from Apollonia, after hearing the news of Caesar's death. The two men had fought Mark Antony, the old order and avenged Caesar's killers together. The loyal lieutenant had orchestrated Octavius' victory at Actium, helping him to win the war - and peace. Agrippa was often called the Second Man of Rome, feared and respected in equal measure, although a recent piece of graffiti Varro had seen in the Subura had satirically suggested that the emperor's wife, Livia, was the Second Man of Rome, given her scope for meddling in the affairs of state (as well as the affairs of her priapic husband). Augustus may have been able to rule an empire, but there were instances where he was unable to rein in his wife. Rumours persisted that the Empress was not averse to employing poison to remove her husband's enemies - and mistresses. There were whispers - no louder than that - that Livia was determined to seat her son (from a previous marriage), Tiberius, on the throne once her husband passed. "Perhaps not even the gods can help anyone who stands in the way of the she-wolf," another piece of graffiti half-jokingly asserted.

There were some who would employ the double-edged compliment and argue that Agrippa was too honourable and decent to be an effective spymaster. But Varro knew how cunning and ruthless he could be, unfortunately. Agrippa also possessed the virtue of being free from vanity, unlike hordes of politicians. Augustus had given his friend a surfeit of power, so he had little appetite to become power-hungry. Agrippa's loyalty to the Emperor was as strong as that of a wife. Or stronger.

Varro's tunic was finely woven and embroidered with gold thread. But it also contained more than one food and wine stain from the party the previous evening. The patrician's hair was unkempt and his eyes as red as a couple carnelian gemstones. The poet, or spy, did his best to suppress another yawn and not throw-up.

Warm air and sunlight poured through the room, along with the fragrances from the flowers – roses, violets, oleanders - in the well-tended garden. Agrippa's shoe tapped upon the tiled floor. He stood in the centre of the room. A couple of praetorian guards, veterans from having campaigned with Agrippa during the civil war, flanked the main entrance to the triclinium. Their frozen expressions could send a chill down one's spine, Varro fancied. Only several cups of warm wine could thaw them out. Another soldier, somewhat younger and more sheepish looking, unobtrusively positioned himself out of the way, next to a marble sculpture of Apollo.

"You seem to have had a long night, Rufus - again," Agrippa remarked, arching a reproving eyebrow.

SPIES OF ROME: BLOOD & POISON

"It already feels like I've had a long life," Varro replied, wearily. He was going to mention how his long life had nearly been cut short on a couple of occasions, thanks to the spymaster's interventions, but he was too tired and thought better of it.

"For once I am going to recommend that you get some rest and go back to sleep. You have a long night ahead, attending another party. Your mission, however, will not be to enjoy yourself."

***

Whilst Fronto arranged some refreshments (soft cheeses and cold meats) for his esteemed guest, Agrippa explained the purpose of his visit. Varro yearned to take the weight off his feet, but he stood to attention in the best fashion he could as he listened to the spymaster:

"Word has reached me of a possible conspiracy. I should say that word often reaches me about possible conspiracies. If I believed every piece of gossip I heard concerning treason and dissent then the population of Rome, or certainly the population of the Senate, would be halved. The only winner would be carpenters, commissioned to produce crucifixes. But we must be vigilant. Most rumours lack substance, but not all. I have heard that Titus Strabo, a scion of one of Rome's ancient families, has a grievance against the Emperor. He wishes to foment trouble - and is aiming to recruit other disgruntled patricians to his cause. Power breeds envy. Strabo is not the first self-regarding statesman from an ancient bloodline who believes he is destined to rule. He doubtless considers that Rome is a prize to be won, rather than an idea to be served. I have received intelligence that Strabo will be meeting with his co-conspirators this evening at a party, hosted by Quintina. Whilst Quintina presides over poetry readings inside, Strabo will be convening a different type of gathering in the garden. I will just need you to venture outside at some point during the night and note those gathered around the senator. You will be familiar with some of the faces. You may have been familiar with their wives and daughters in the past. You will not be considered an uninvited or unsurprising guest at the gathering. You are already acquainted with Quintina, no?"

"Yes, I am acquainted with Quintina. She is a woman of great riches, but little taste. The two do not go together as often as you might think. There was a time when she desired to get further acquainted with me, although I suspect that you already know that."

Varro pictured the hostess of one of Rome's most prestigious literary salons. Quintina was middle-aged, but the years had been kind to the celebrated beauty. The daughter of a humble stablemaster had married - and divorced - well over the past decade. She had invested intelligently and amassed a small fortune. Quintina was now famous, or infamous, for collecting young poets the way the Empress collected poisons, or her husband collected mistresses. Varro had been one of the few poets in Rome to refuse the advances of the attractive patroness (he was not in need of funds and was happily married to his wife, Lucilla, at the time - which is not to say that he wasn't unfaithful on other occasions). Every month the "literary lioness" arranged a lavish party, involving delicacies from the city's best cooks, fine wines and, unfortunately, poetry readings. Young writers, craving patronage or praise, would compete for Quintina's affections like chicks singing in the nest to attract the attention of their mother to give them food.

"You are, as I understand it, one of the ones which got away. You still remain outside her stable of authors, which only makes her want you to enter her circle more, so to speak. She is still an admirer of yours."

"As I said, Quintina doesn't necessarily possess the best taste. I dare say that she considers me too old now to satisfy her appetites. She prefers fresh talent. Ripe, or under ripe, fruit."

"But she will welcome you with open arms. No one will bat an eyelid at your presence at the party. I cannot foresee that there will be any threat to your person this evening," Agrippa said with confidence. Varro raised a sceptical rather than reproving eyebrow in reply. "I understand that your bodyguard, Manius, is still away from the city with his new wife. As such I have arranged for Felix here to serve as your attendant. He is the nephew of a fine soldier I once fought beside. He had one of the best bow arms in the army. He was a good friend - and I do not forget my friends. Unfortunately for my enemies, I remember them too."

The young man, standing next to the sculpture of Apollo, stood a little more dutifully on hearing his name being called. His body stiffened to attention, and he thrust out his chest. Muscles bulged beneath a freshly laundered tunic. He had the build of a veteran, but almost comically boyish features - full of hope and an eagerness to please.

Varro's sense of hope and willingness to please were less apparent. But he would accede to the request - or rather order - to attend the party that evening.

***

The light was fading, the temperature beginning to drop. But plenty of people still populated the streets of the Palatine hill - patricians and plebs alike. Perspiring, careworn litter bearers. Messengers, hastily weaving their way through the throng. Elegant women, dressed in shimmering, silk stolas - with attendants following in their wake, burdened with shopping like pack animals. Self-important government officials, stroking their beards and trading gossip.

Felix, accompanying Varro, was now out of uniform. In order to justify carrying his bow he was dressed like he had spent the day hunting. As well as a couple of dead woodpigeons, he carried in his bag a dozen arrows and a hunting knife. The young soldier gripped his bow and kept his eyes alert for any threats. He was keen to impress. Felix's worry, perhaps more than being attacked, was that he would dishonour his family and family name if he failed in his duty.

"Agrippa speaks highly of you, Felix. You may only be now able to disappoint him," Varro remarked, amusing himself by witnessing the concern etched into the adolescent's features. "I am joking, of course. It pains me to observe such a serious face on such young shoulders. It seems that you have decided to become a careerist soldier, no?"

"It's my ambition to one day serve in the Praetorian Guard."

"I envy your sense of purpose. The most I can aspire to be is a wastrel. The only thing I need to wake up for in the morning is to have an afternoon nap later in the day. But being a poet is not without its perils. We are sensitive and often have our hearts broken by our muses. The curvaceous can turn into the callous, with just one misplaced word. Many a mistress can leave you with the love token of the pox or, worse, fall in love with you. Critics may not necessarily draw blood, but they can stab you in the back quicker than you can unleash an arrow. Hopefully my verse isn't so powerful, or the women so amorous, that I will need a bodyguard at the party tonight. You will be waiting around for a long time, for nothing. You can take the evening off, Felix. That's an order."

***

A sea of people bustled and swayed throughout the opulent reception room. Patrons of the arts. Posturing poets. Wives and daughters, simpering before the same men. Merchants. The senatorial class. The amount of perfume wafting around made Varro's eyes water. Dramatic dresses - and hairstyles - were on display in an unofficial contest. Whispers and laughter filled the air, along with the melodic sound of one of Rome's most famed harp players. The drink and conversation flowed. Varro positioned himself in the corner so that he could keep an eye on anyone slipping out into the garden, although there were other exits that the spy was unable to observe.

The wine was easier to swallow than the poetry. The verse lacked rhythm and satire. It was all far too earnest and turgid. Too many of the poets wished to signal how virtuous they were. Progressive. Too many of the poems began with the word "I". Varro thought how he would have been irritated if compelled to recite some of his verses as well, yet he would also be offended if he was not invited to do so. The charming, wealthy patrician exchanged pleasantries and gossip, salacious or otherwise, with plenty of acquaintances. People enjoyed Varro's sharp tongue, so long as it wasn't directed at them. He could be witty and self-effacing (although self-effacing could turn into self-loathing sometimes in private).

SPIES OF ROME: BLOOD & POISON

"What a pleasant surprise," Quintina pronounced, as the hostess made her way over to Varro's corner of the room. "We haven't seen you here for some months. Have you been locking yourself away to write, or making your mark in some other fashion, Rufus?"

Quintina eyed her guest up and down, as if appraising a statue she might bid upon. Varro was more subtle when taking in the woman's expensive dress, made from Chinese silk, and even more expensive jewellery (which was just about the right side of gaudy). He was not sure whether her make-up distracted from or highlighted her advancing years.

"I've been expending a considerable amount of energy avoiding any work, as usual," Varro replied, unsheathing his second-best disarming smile. The spy wondered if Quintina could be part of any conspiracy. Women were as much capable of duplicity as men, if not more so, Varro judged. Yet she had always been a supporter and admirer of the Emperor. Rumour had it that she once enjoyed a dalliance with Augustus, when she was married. He seemed to find the wives of other men far more attractive than other available women. It was a form of sport for the Emperor to steal them away for a night or month, just to show that he could.

"Thankfully your former wife isn't so idle. Lucilla kindly provided me with some valuable financial advice the other day. She is a wise woman. It is a shame that the treasury does not employ her to counsel them, although I sense she is the wrong sex - and not sufficiently corrupt - to prosper there."

"You are looking well Quintina," Varro replied, keen to veer the conversation away from his former wife.

"I hope so. I certainly paid my dressmaker and hairdresser enough to turn some heads. But what do you think of the poets you have heard so far this evening? Darius could be a talent - if he would let me guide him. It is a shame that you never entered my circle, Rufus."

"I'm afraid that it is just one of many regrets I have, in relation to my writing career. The list is growing as long as *The Iliad*, I warrant."

Varro remembered how keen Quintina was for him to submit to her - and follow her advice - when he was a young poet. "You have potential," she had commented, which was a double-edged compliment if ever he heard one. Varro had spurned her offer - and the woman felt slighted, albeit not for long. He had dedicated a poem to her, swapping out the name of a previous mistress for hers in a poem he had composed in his youth. But Quintina had proved herself genuinely generous, as well genuinely lustful, in her pursuit of fostering talent. Varro had known patrons who had been far more abusive and controlling in their relationships with poets and artists.

"You have gathered quite a crowd," Varro added, pretending to survey the room whilst examining if anyone was venturing out into the garden for a clandestine meeting.

"Aside from desiring to be rich and powerful, Rome's elite like to be cultured. Or just to be seen as being cultured. I should say I saw you last evening, at Luca's party. You were being less than cultured with a young woman. Did you enjoy yourself?" Quintina said, raising her eyebrow, suggestively.

"It was a night to remember."

***

Quintina soon fluttered off to attend to other guests, like a moth attracted to a brighter flame. It was time for Varro to discover whether it was going to be an evening to remember or forget. There was every possibility that Agrippa's intelligence could prove but a rumour and he would encounter a courting couple in the garden rather than any sinister conspirators. His plan was to just innocently wander outside with a winecup in his hand and pretend to take some air whilst being half-drunk.

He ventured out into the garden, appreciating the cool breeze on his flushed face. A plump moon and a cloudless sky, freckled with stars, greeted him. Varro witnessed a few spectral figures move around at the bottom of the garden. He walked past various statues, across the manicured lawn. There was a table, containing a wine jug, and half a dozen men standing around. A couple of braziers lit and heated the scene, although the scene was still washed in a stygian gloom.

SPIES OF ROME: BLOOD & POISON

With one hand Varro wiped his perspiring palm on his tunic - and with the other he drained his cup. He recognised the familiar voice before he could clearly see the familiar face. The spy did his best to ensure that his features didn't betray the chill he felt in his heart.

"Please, sit. You were expecting someone else, no?" Publius Dio remarked, convivially. "I would have been surprised, however, if Agrippa dispatched anyone else but your good self. We are at a gathering for Rome's literary set - and you are familiar with the good and the great. Please, do sit Rufus. Forgive my deception in drawing you here this evening. All will be well, I promise. I want to make you an offer you can't refuse."

Varro's eyes flitted from side to side as he surveyed Dio's lantern-jawed bodyguards - former gladiators who appeared even less garrulous and more humourless than Agrippa's attendants - before taking a seat opposite at the marble-topped table.

Publius Dio. Smuggler. Moneylender. Merchant. Murderer. Torturer. Dio considered himself a facilitator, who would happily arrange anything - including virginal girls, rare animals worth hunting and deadly poisons for family members to use on one another - so long as the price was right. He was not beyond bribing or blackmailing government officials - or removing them from their office through more drastic means if called for. Dio possessed friends in high places, including the Empress, to furnish him with a certain degree of influence and immunity.

"Like our hostess, I know how to identify and reward talent," Dio added. "I can understand why Agrippa recruited you. You can move easily in different social circles. You are an astute judge of character - and I do not say this just because you befriended me all those years ago. Agrippa is probably aware of how you can have the ear, heart and other body parts of the wives of Rome's elite. Yes, Agrippa did well to recruit you. But I would warn you not to be taken in by him. The warmonger has more blood on his hands than I could manage in ten lifetimes. I imagine that he would have waxed lyrical about you doing your duty when he first approached you. There were enemies of the state that he implored you to help defeat, no? You would make your father proud if you served Rome. I am all too familiar with his pitch. Agrippa has recruited many a spy, chewed them up and spat them out. He is the arch-manipulator, arch-deceiver. He will not spare you a second thought should you become compromised, and you end up at the bottom of the Tiber. There may be plenty of currency in Agrippa's flattery and talk of courage and duty. But the only currency is currency. You may already consider yourself wealthy, Rufus. But more is more. Should you permit me to be your new patron I can help you fund a political campaign. You will be able to ascend the course of honours, leapfrogging your rivals. We will be able to do great things together. Politicians, not poets, can change the world for the better. Crime pays. Or rather, instead of crime, it's about embracing a sense of enterprise. Agrippa is accustomed to spying on others. It's about time someone spied on him. Who better than a poet to deliver some poetic justice?"

Varro remained largely impassive as Dio spoke, aside from a wry flicker of a smile at the end. Even the spy didn't know if he feigned the gesture or was being genuine. Life still had the ability to surprise, as opposed to bore him. He took a breath, took a swig of wine, and replied:

"You may be over-estimating my value to the Second Man of Rome. I'm not sure if I am even of secondary importance to Agrippa. I'm certainly not privy to his plans and who else he has recruited. I'm a reluctant spy, at best. I will make an even more reluctant politician. I'm not sufficiently dishonourable to engage with the course of honours. Even I may possess too many morals to enter politics. But you have given me some food for thought, far more than any poet inside has. I am not wedded to serving Agrippa or Rome. I do not have the energy to be an idealogue. You know me to be more self-serving than that. You will understand if I am wary of switching horses in mid-stream. The last time we encountered one another you threatened to kill me. Now you are promising fortune and glory."

"The fault was mine. Forgive me. My blood boiled over. Remember that an old and trusted friend - who was dear to me, who I had shared many a mistress and jug of wine with - had just betrayed me to my enemy. I can assure you, Rufus, that I wish you no harm. Indeed, the opposite is true. I want us to be friends and business associates. I will be the first to injure anyone who even thinks about causing you harm."

Dio poured out another couple of measures of wine. He smiled and his features softened, although his eyes remained shrewd and obsidian-hard as he scrutinised Varro for any indicators of interest. The criminal preferred operating in the shadows and avoiding exposure, but it was worth rolling the dice to secure an asset inside of Agrippa's inner circle. The better informed he was, the better informed his decisions would be. Dio believed that he remained one step ahead of the likes of Agrippa and his rivals. But two steps ahead would be preferable, more profitable, he reasoned.

"You have certainly presented me with an offer that I will think about. Forgive me if I do not make a hasty decision either way. I may not be interested in making speeches as a politician, but money talks. My divorce settlement sometimes feels as punitive as Rome's punishment towards Carthage. I would be interested in discussing the issue some more, in relation to the terms of any agreement and any remuneration. I can appreciate that crime pays. But how much?"

Dio grinned and clapped his hands. Pleased. Applauding.

"Crime will pay even more if you don a toga and join the Senate. Your father's name will earn you sufficient votes to ensure your candidacy. But I understand if you want to sleep on any decision."

The two men finished off the jug of wine. Varro praised the vintage. Dio boasted how he had a special deal with his wine merchant. They gossiped about mutual acquaintances and vented spleen and satire. They fraternally clasped one another's forearm in a Roman handshake before Varro finally took his leave.

"I'm tempted, Publius. More than tempted," Varro remarked, looking his potential confederate squarely in the eye.

He was convincing, Dio thought. *But not convincing enough. Well played, Rufus. But you still have a shred of decency and honour left in you, unfortunately. It was a source of weakness way back when, as it is now. If you're not for me, you're against me. You are not the only astute judge of character. I can read you, as easily as I can your poems. A man's eyes are a window into his soul. I could see how tempted you really were. It is not only women who do not like being spurned.*

Publius Dio's entire face now hardened. His hand tightened around his winecup as if it were a claw or talon. With just a slight nod of his head he beckoned over his bodyguard, Milo.

"See that he doesn't get home safely," Dio ordered, his voice as hard as his countenance. "Take two men. Have it appear like a robbery. Make it quick and painless. The man used to be a friend of mine. I am not completely devoid of compassion."

***

The night nearly swallowed him up. Thankfully the moon was full, and the residents of Palatine could afford to burn oil lamps in their gardens throughout the night. Varro was no stranger to staggering back through the neighbourhood in the middle of the evening. Unlike the Subura at this time - with its revellers either venturing home or moving on to the next tavern or brothel - the Palatine was quiet.

The spy hoped that he had been convincing enough. If he had been too eager to accept Dio's proposal, then he would have been suspicious. A flat refusal might have provoked an adverse reaction too. Varro smiled at the thought of acting as Dio's proxy - puppet - in the Senate. His life was comic or tragic enough, without having to strut out onto the political stage. It would have hurt his head and been exhausting to play a double or triple agent, he fancied. Out of fear, or perhaps a sense of duty and honour, Varro had no intention of betraying Agrippa. The spymaster had been responsible for nearly getting him killed on one occasion, but Agrippa had also saved his life. It was an easy decision to make, to side with the second most powerful man in Rome. He did not feel any desire to become Dio's ally. Varro would have preferred, of course, not to work for either party.

His ears became attuned to the sound of footsteps behind him. Varro suddenly found himself missing his friend and bodyguard, Manius, more keenly. The spy quickened his pace. But so did his

SPIES OF ROME: BLOOD & POISON

pursuers. It could be nothing, he told himself. Spying breeds paranoia. But then again...

The smuggler had employed Milo as much for his compliant attitude as for his skills. He never baulked at obeying an order, even if it meant disfiguring a woman or murdering a child. Whether he killed in or out of the arena made little, if any, difference to the fearsome gladiator. His face and body were marked with a wince-inducing sum of welts and scars. A bite-sized chunk was missing from his left earlobe and his right jaw was covered with either a birth or burn mark. One wouldn't want to meet the enforcer on a dark night, which Varro was about to do. Milo, after receiving the spy's address from his employer, instructed one of his men - Valerian - to run and get in front of their quarry. He knew the spot where he would ambush the patrician. The spy was as good as dead.

The street was narrow, no wider the length of a horse from head to tail. The walls of properties on both sides were too high to scale. A breathless Valerian appeared at the far end of the street, a club in hand. Varro recognised the bodyguard from earlier. The spy turned around to see another two opponents approaching from the other end of the street. There would be no escape. Fight or die. Or both. His heart was racing. His legs would need too as well, soon. Varro shivered. His sun-kissed complexion grew pale. He willed himself to remember the training Manius had given him over the years. He wasn't the worst poet to call upon in a fight, but that was scarce a boast. His best option would be to engage the solitary man ahead of him, do enough to get past the brute and retreat. He cursed Dio. He cursed himself for instructing Felix to leave his post. But he didn't want the young man to waste his evening, waiting around. But it would have been good training for the soldier. To wait. Varro turned to address Milo, who was better dressed than his confederates and possessed an air of authority.

"I don't suppose I could interest you in a bribe?"

Milo shook his head and grinned, revealing an absence of front teeth. No doubt he was missing a sense of clemency too. The bodyguard drew a well-used but well-maintained gladius. The similarly unpleasant figure next to Milo drew his weapon. Ready and willing to use it. Varro drew his small knife. It was better than nothing, but not by much.

The three men closed on their target. Victim.

A strange sound curdled the air. Milo's grin turned into a grimace and his body twisted, as if he were possessed by an evil spirit, before falling to the ground. The sound grew familiar, however, as Varro heard it a second time. The twang of a bowstring, succeeded by an arrow thudding into flesh. The thug alongside Milo fell too as Varro observed the figure of Felix at the end of the street.

Footsteps alerted the spy to the approaching assailant. The archer had now no line of sight, as Varro stood in front on his attacker. Instinct or training kicked in as Varro reached up and caught his opponent's arm, before Valerian could bring his club down. The bodyguard expected his opponent to try and stab him in the chest - but Varro plunged the blade into his groin. The pain was more than mildly unpleasant. The spy, possessed by a rare moment of bloodlust, proceeded to bury the knife in the enforcer's neck. Blood gushed out, like vomit.

Felix was soon by Varro's side, an arrow nocked in readiness. But the fight was over. The young soldier's heart was still galloping. He had only ever killed animals before or shot at wooden targets. It was a lot to take in. But he had done his job. Done his duty.

"I've never been so thankful for someone disobeying my instructions before," Varro remarked, catching his breath.

"With all due respect, I thought it best to follow Agrippa's orders, who told me to keep an eye on you no matter what."

"All's well that ends well, Felix. But let us hope things do not now end well for Publius Dio."

***

Varro returned home, torn between shock and anger. Fronto dispatched a slave to send a message to Marcus Agrippa. The slave returned with a dozen soldiers.

Agrippa arrived at first light. Varro couldn't quite tell if the spymaster was upset because he had been duped by the smuggler, or because Dio had dared to attempt to eliminate one of his agents.

"You did well, Rufus. You too Felix," the statesman remarked. With what little energy the young soldier had left, having served as a sentry all night, Felix thrust out his chest once more and beamed with pride. "Tell me, were you not tempted by Dio's offer?"

"I am much more suited for running away than running for office. Even before the evidence of this evening, I knew that Dio would prove a false friend. Besides, I enjoy working for you too much," Varro ended with, not a little sarcastically.

"I'm happy to hear it, as there is more work to be done. It's kill or be killed now. His relationship with the Empress may spare him from being prosecuted through the courts - but there are other forms of justice. In deciding to murder one of my agents, the cur signed his own death sentence. I do not forget my friends - and I remember my enemies," Agrippa said, determinedly. "We just have to find the snake again. The smuggler is adept at hiding himself away."

"I believe I can find him," Varro replied, recalling how Dio had mentioned the name of a wine merchant who regularly supplied him with various vintages. The spy smiled, with not a little satisfaction.

He's as good as dead.

RICHARD FOREMAN

Blood & Poison

Rufus Varro yawned and rubbed his eyes. No matter how late in the day Marcus Agrippa called upon him, he always considered it too early. The two men stood in the aristocrat's triclinium, one appearing more dishevelled than the other. Varro's unruly black curls hung down, covering the scar on his forehead (a memento from a previous mission the reluctant spy had carried out for the Second man of Rome). His red-rimmed eyes were still tired from staying up late and reading - and his head ached from too much wine.

"For all intents and purposes, I'm not here," Agrippa remarked, pretending not to notice the various food stains down his agent's tunic.

"I know that I had a few drinks last night, but I don't believe I'm seeing things," Varro replied, thinking how he wished that Agrippa wasn't really present and it was all a dream - as the spymaster's visits were often a prelude to him nearly being killed.

An unamused Agrippa rolled his eyes - and ignored the droll comment. He wanted to discuss the business at hand, promptly, and move onto his next appointment. Agrippa wasn't one to tarry and trade meaningless gossip. It was said that he could design and construct a building in the same span of time that the Senate could discuss its planning permission.

"I have come about our wine merchant, Gaius Vettius. One of my agents has confirmed his whereabouts. He is currently residing at his property in Arretium. As much as the merchant might value Dio's custom, Vettius is far more loyal to himself. I have a letter here which will duly inspire a sense of fear and greed in him. I believe that Vettius will cooperate and sell out Dio quicker than he would export a consignment of Falernian. Once you have gained Dio's location from the merchant, you should proceed to apprehend him. As well as letting Felix accompany you, I will grant you the necessary authority to call upon any nearby army camp and sequester any and all resources and personnel. Dio will doubtless have a small force of bodyguards and former gladiators travelling with him in his retinue. Things could, or will, get bloody."

"And what should I do with Dio, if I'm able to apprehend him?"

"Kill him, Rufus. Because if you do not, he will arrange to kill you. It would not surprise me if he has already arranged for someone to abduct or assassinate you. You're a piece of unfinished business. His aim will probably be to torture you first. I will spare you the gory details, you are a poet and have imagination enough. But the brief is not to bring the snake to Rome, to stand trial. We cannot rely on the courts. Justice can be bought in Rome, as one might buy a house or roasted pig. The bigger the fish, the easier it can slip through the net. Dio has friends in high places," Agrippa asserted, without mentioning the name of the Emperor's wife. Livia.

Agrippa had no need to mention her name, however. Varro was all too aware of how the "First Woman of Rome" (although some jokingly dubbed her the Second Man of Rome, much to Agrippa's chagrin) had recently purchased a consignment of the poison, Nightshade, from Dio. The poison, seemingly concocted in Hades, was tasteless, odourless and deadly. Livia had granted the smuggler immunity from prosecution, when Agrippa had apprehended him before. Varro recalled a piece of graffiti he had seen recently (which was quickly scrubbed clean away) positing that Livia had no need to keep the priapic Augustus in her bed, because she had him in the palm of her hand. Varro wondered who the Empress was intending to use the Nightshade on. Agrippa had once mentioned how the woman kept one eye on the past, righting the wrongs of those who had opposed her. And one eye on the future, to secure the succession of her son, Tiberius. Rumour had it that Livia often acted as a pimp to her husband's mistresses, so they would not prove a genuine rival or threat.

"Death comes to everyone, but it can't come soon enough to Dio," Agrippa added, his face contorting into an uncharacteristic sneer. Varro imagined that the spymaster's professional pride was still smarting. Not only had Dio outmanoeuvred him to escape capture, but the smuggler had dared to attempt to assassinate one of his agents.

Dio had been a drinking companion of the aristocrat in his youth. The two friends had shared many a jug of expensive wine and cheap whores together. Dio had somewhat annulled any affection he had for his old friend by giving an order to kill him the other evening. They had crossed the Rubicon. One of them had to die for the other to live. Rufus Varro glanced at a bust of his stoical father. The senator had been a devoted servant to Rome. The son wondered how proud or ashamed his father would be if he knew that the once promising poet had become a spy - and now assassin.

"You will forgive me if I write my will before I set off - and understand if I do not bequeath anything to you," Varro, perhaps only half-jokingly, remarked.

Agrippa permitted himself a flicker of a grim smile. But his features then became as stony as the bust of his host's father.

"You will have the advantage of surprise. You will also possess a small army of soldiers, should you need them. I have every confidence in you, Rufus."

"I wish I shared your confidence."

"There are those with fewer abilities who have achieved more."

"I don't suppose that they are somehow available for the mission? I will duly reward them handsomely should they be willing to take my place," Varro remarked, again only half-jokingly.

Out the corner of his eye he observed Felix. The young soldier was out of uniform, but as ready as ever to do his duty. Felix shuffled on his feet, either nervous or excited, like a horse about to take part in a chariot race.

"More than anyone else, you have the means and motivation to complete the mission," Agrippa argued. For once, Varro was unable to argue back.

***

His mood - and arse - were sore. Save for a brief respite when they fed and watered their horses, Varro had been in the saddle for most of the day. And they were still a couple of days ride from reaching their destination. A burning blue firmament, worthy of a poetic description, shone overhead. Clouds, lazier than Varro, ambled from east to west. The landscape was a sea of vineyards, pasture and olive groves. Plumes of smoke, from tanneries, bakeries and houses, wended their way skywards, breaking up the line of the horizon. Varro fancied how he should now be relaxing in his garden on such a fine day, reading or idly (very idly) composing a poem. Fronto should soon be coming out onto the lawn, either to re-fill his wine jug or ask him what his cook should rustle up for lunch.

All roads lead to Rome. People were drawn to the city, like flies to shit. Most of the traffic which Varro and Felix encountered, as they ventured northwards towards Arretium, was travelling in the opposite direction. Merchants and carters were laden with wares to sell in the capital. Groups of soldiers kicked up dust. Most were square-jawed, grim-faced. But some smiled to themselves, wondering which drinking holes and brothels they might frequent in the Subura by nightfall. A few carriages passed Varro - as the aristocrat thought how they might contain his neighbours from the Palatine Hill (not that he was in a mood to stop and gossip). Leather-faced yokels trundled by too, hoping to find their fortune in Rome. They would more likely find misfortune, Varro fancied.

Felix rode ahead, keener than his companion to complete his mission. The soldier wanted to prove himself, to Agrippa, his family and the world. He had spent the previous evening sharpening his sword and checking the points and feathers on his arrows. Felix yearned to serve the empire, vanquish its enemies and earn enough coin to purchase some land after retiring. Or he aimed to serve in the Praetorian Guard.

Varro had grown fond of the lad - and not just because Felix had saved his life. The youthful soldier was old enough to kill - but also old enough to die. The spy felt a responsibility towards his dutiful bodyguard. Varro decided to engage the youth in conversation again, to help pass the time and get to know his companion.

"So, Felix, do you have a woman back in Rome?"

The virginal soldier blushed.

"I can only admire her from afar," Felix sheepishly replied, as he thought about Sabina. She was the daughter of a senator. The politician would often arrange for soldiers to serve as his daughter's bodyguards. Sabina treated Felix differently, compared to the other soldiers. She spoke to him differently. Looked at him differently. As much as his heart and ardour might soar when he pictured Sabina, his thoughts became grounded when he realised that the girl would soon be wed. The senator was keen to marry his daughter into a powerful, patrician family. "I have acted honourably towards her. Sometimes my thoughts have been dishonourable, though."

Varro smiled. The youth was worthy of satire and sympathy.

"Ah, dishonourable thoughts. The best kind of thoughts. You could be a poet, possessed by such unrequited love. But let us arrange some requited lust. I know a place where you will be able to forget about your muse. The wine will taste like the waters of Lethe. If memory serves there is a house of ill repute, which is of good repute, on our way to Arretium. I have enough coin to purchase you passage to Elysium and back."

"But what about our mission?" Felix exclaimed, torn between duty and pleasure.

"The mission can wait half a day. Or night."

***

The road was long. As the horses bowed their heads in tiredness, the two riders bowed their heads in thought.

The plan was simple, Varro mused. Find the wine merchant. Extract Dio's location from him. Travel to where the smuggler was hiding. Muster an army from the closest encampment and defeat Dio and his force of bodyguards and gladiators. Execute his former friend, if he fails to die during the fighting. The plan was simple. But life was often more complicated.

The spy was mindful of not underestimating Dio, partly because he had done so before. The smuggler was always one step ahead - and thought two moves ahead. "The bastard is as slippery as an eel, covered in oil," Varro had said to Fronto, before setting off. There was a lot that remained unsaid between the aristocrat and his paternalistic estate manager, as they stood outside the house. During the night Varro had composed letters to Fronto, Manius and Lucilla. He prayed that they would not need to break the seals on the scrolls, but prayers often went unanswered. The gods could be even more indifferent than the poet.

"This may well be the last time you suffer my company," the Roman remarked, appearing uncharacteristically vulnerable and emotional. "I should say -"

"You should say nothing," Fronto interjected, his voice croaky with age or sentiment. "I'm far too stubborn to allow you not to outlive me."

"But if you tell Lucilla to -"

"You can tell her yourself, when you return. This game that you have been drawn into with Dio, I have every confidence that you will win in the end. You are proving yourself to be an adept spy. You have been deceiving yourself for most of your life. I do not see why you will not be able to deceive and best Dio too."

"Thank you, I think," Varro responded, just about holding back the tears or laughter.

***

Dusk was slipping into night, like grains of sands falling through an hourglass. Varro's arse ached all the more - but his mood became less sore upon spying the settlement in the distance. The dissolute poet had visited the renowned brothel before. *The Sacred Hart* was the only establishment of its kind in the immediate area. Unlike the Subura, where venues would compete on price - and it was a race to the bottom, so to speak – *The Sacred Hart* charged more for its wares. But, like so much in life, you get what you pay for, Varro mused.

The brothel was located within a short distance of a town, army camp and a host of properties owned by plutocrats and politicians (the latter may have even purchased second homes in the area to be close to the establishment). The oldest profession was still going strong.

The young man's eyes were as bright as the oil lamps burning on the horizon. The mission - and Sabina - were even further from his mind. He felt a mixture of both nervousness and excitement - or lustiness. He began to imagine the flesh on show. His stomach rumbled, but something other than feeling famished made him kick his heels into the sides of his mount to quicken his pace. A couple of phalluses carved into the road would point the way to their destination, if his companion somehow forgot the route.

A flicker of a smile appeared on Varro's face as he witnessed Felix's walk turn into a trot. He wouldn't be surprised if the trot soon turned into a full-bloodied gallop.

***

After an attendant saw to their horses, they entered the reception area of the establishment. A couple of braziers, flanking the doorway, ensured a warm welcome. The young soldier's senses were immediately assaulted by the smell of perfume, the sound of a harp playing and the arresting sight of a half-dressed Nubian girl in charge of relieving patrons of their weapons. Altercations inevitably ensued when one mixed men, wine and whores. It was best that such fights were conducted with fists rather than blades. The various ex-gladiators who stood sentry-like around the venue were quick to eject any miscreants, however. Felix's attention was also naturally attracted to the curtain, separating the reception area from the main chamber - he caught a glimpse of a veritable banquet of girls. The soldier had frequented plenty of drinking houses and even brothels before - but he had never visited such a salubrious establishment.

Valeria, who managed the brothel, offered up a warm welcome too as she greeted the patrons. Varro remembered the hostess from previous visits. She was a little plumper than before - and could only just carry off the dresses and jewellery which former lovers and customers had gifted to her when younger. Her make-up was nearly as thick as her waist, the satirical poet unfairly judged. Valeria had been in the trade since she was fifteen. She was now approaching fifty. She had nearly married at twenty-five when a regular customer, who was as rich as Crassus (well, half as rich but that was more than enough), told her that he would devote himself to her for the rest of her life. That she was the only woman he had ever loved. Shortly before the wedding day Valeria discovered that her prospective husband had been married four times - and had left his previous wives in penury. As if she didn't know already, the prostitute realised than men lied, as surely as they breathed. Valeria was wise beyond her years. She knew who was likely to get drunk and rowdy - and who was likely to get drunk and randy. She had a memory for the names and appetites of her regulars. The hostess knew what her customers wanted before they did. Despite having lived a life full of bruises and bouts of the pox Valeria was quick to laugh and smile - and even quicker to take a customer's money. She had an array of scornful and withering looks for any guests who tried to haggle over prices.

"Welcome, gentlemen. And how can we help you this evening? Are you interested in some wine or women?" she asked, having a vague memory of having met one of the patrons before. She recalled that he was not short of courteousness or coin.

Varro was so exhausted that he was tempted to ask for an empty bed for the night, just so he could sleep. He was unsure whether he could raise a smile, let alone anything else. But he was thirsty and mindful of staying up to look after his companion.

"Without wanting to sound too greedy, we're interested in both. Some food wouldn't go amiss too."

"You're a man after my own heart," Valeria replied. "Have you been to *The Sacred Hart* before?"

"Aye, which is why I was keen to come again. You'll be pleased to hear that I've got more money than sense. But, rather than myself, I'd like you to look after my young friend here."

Varro made a generous downpayment to show his intent and allowed for the Nubian to take his sword and dagger. Felix became suitable glassy-eyed and slack-jawed when he was led through the curtain. Erotic art, containing contorted bodies and enormous heads, adorned the walls. Semi-precious baubles sparkled in the soft light. Bronzed flesh shone, along with shimmering silks. Lighter chimed, in tune with clinking cups. Felix blushed - his skin the colour of the wine which a lissom serving girl handed to him - and took in the scene. He felt like he had gone through a door into another world. Elysium. Varro took in the scene and felt at home.

"It will be his first time," he discreetly remarked to the hostess. "I trust you have a girl who will be gentle with him, so to speak."

"Don't worry, dear. He will be in good hands, so to speak."

After seating her new customers in a booth in the corner, Valeria whispered into a young girl's ear and nodded in Felix's direction. She was sweet-faced, for a whore, Varro thought. The hostess had chosen well. Certainly Felix had no complaints when the hostess introduced him to Fulvia. She wore a long dress with an unsubtle slit, which ran all the way up to Elysium. Her tanned mid-rift was bare and Felix found himself naval-gazing, when his eyes were not devouring the rest of the nubile girl's assets. Varro encouraged his friend to abandon him for the company of girl. The sinewy Athenian led the soldier off - and he duly followed her like a puppy dog, tossing her head back and laughing playfully at something the customer said as she did so. She sat him down and ordered a couple of expensive drinks. She would not rush things. Valeria quietly mentioned that his companion had deep pockets. Fulvia quite liked first timers. They could be a bit awkward and clumsy, but they were often respectful and tipped well.

Varro clasped his half empty winecup (or Fronto would argue that it should be considered half full) and surveyed the scene. Despite it being relatively early the establishment was already busy. Most of the bedrooms were located on the first floor. Varro noted the constant creaking of the stairs as a constant stream of whores and customers travelled up and down. Each narrow room would contain a bed, toilet pot, water jug and some wine. Unlike many low-rent brothels, which the aristocrat tended to avoid nowadays, the walls between rooms did not just consist of a worn, stained curtain. As usual, there were plenty of soldiers decamping for the night (albeit they were officers, as the prices would be prohibitive for the average, low-ranking legionary). Plenty of affluent greybeards were in situ. The regulars seemed to have their preferred booths and girls. Money was placed into perfumed palms and hands were slid up tunics and dresses. Brothels were named "wolf-dens". Many a patron visited an establishment thinking that he was a predator - but in truth they were the prey.

Quite a few comely whores tried to catch Varro's eye, and some approached the monied stranger, but he smiled politely and gently shook his head to indicate that he wasn't interested. Instead of any musky perfume he welcomed the smells coming from the kitchen. While Felix continued with his courtship of Fulvia, Varro tucked into a pork chop, having been initially tempted by the red mullet. The meat may have been as tough as old leather, but it still filled a hole.

As at home as the Roman felt in the den of iniquity, he felt a twinge of sorrow and regret as he remembered how, for a time, he had felt at home with Lucilla. He would happily spend his days and evenings with his wife. Reading. Writing. Conversing. Eating meals she cooked. Making love. The poet had been the author of his own misery, however. He was well versed in secrets and lies well before Agrippa had employed him as a spy. Varro eventually remained as faithful as a whore - and the considerable amount of wine he consumed couldn't wash away his guilt. The aristocrat had seemingly devoted his life to various pleasures - women, wine and song. The Epicureans argued that "Pleasure was the beginning and end of living happily". But how truly happy had Varro been, he asked himself, before or after his marriage to Lucilla?

***

Felix certainly appeared happy as he descended the stairs with Fulvia. He was a tad wobbly-legged and glazed with sweat. Varro wondered if he had worn the same idiotic grin on his face when a courtesan had turned him into a man (or slavering beast) years ago. Probably. Hopefully he had experienced some dishonourable acts with the whore, rather than just thoughts.

The soldier glanced over at Varro but the older man just raised his cup in a toast and nodded that he was fine to remain on his own, as the girl intended to lead him off into the corner for another overpriced drink. But they never got there.

"This one's mine," Titus Cotta exclaimed, as his flabby fingers clasped Fulvia's arm, and wine dribbled down his chin. The local official was a regular customer - and often picked Fulvia to spend the night with him. None of the girls, or other customers, particularly liked the boorish administrator who had previously served as a tax collector. He had paid a bribe to secure the position - and duly skimmed off the top to reimburse himself for his investment. There was a marked discrepancy between how important he thought he was and how important he actually was. Cotta owned a balding head, pot belly, pinched features and furtive eyes. He had often misled other people - and so was wary of being misled in return. The corrupt official, if we cannot deem that a tautology, was not averse to receiving a bribe (especially when he suggested it). Cotta was servile to his superiors but a tyrant towards those beneath him in rank.

Felix was unschooled in the etiquette of such places, but his father had raised him to stand up and defend a woman's honour (even if some might have judged that the whore had little honour left). He removed Cotta's paw and fronted up to the official, his broad chest in stark contrast to the bureaucrat's paunch.

"How dare you! You insolent dog!" Cotta barked, flanked by two burly attendants. "Do you know who I am?" the imperial administrator added, puffing out what little chest he possessed.

"No, nor do I wish to know," Varro replied, inserting himself into the scene. He didn't want his friend to have a night to remember for all the wrong reasons. "A sense of self-importance is nothing to boast about."

"I could make your life a misery," Catta warned, near snarling, considering himself a law unto himself in the area. Valeria gave him leeway in the establishment, knowing that he could make her life difficult by extorting money or closing the brothel down.

"You already are," Varro wryly countered, taking in the two bodyguards. They were getting old and growing too fat, but he still would have preferred Manius by his side. The satirical aristocrat had lost count of the sum of times that the Briton had extricated them both from trouble, which Varro had plunged them into when drunk.

The tension in the air increased, like clouds congealing before a storm. A fair few patrons turned their heads, some pleased that the stranger was standing up to the petty, vindictive official.

Sensing an altercation, Valeria was also quick on the scene. Desiring to put out any fire before it started. A subtle darting of her eyes also indicated for a couple of attendants to accompany her.

"Gentlemen, I hope all is well here," the hostess said with a broad, emollient smile. It was not the first time that Cotta had caused a disturbance at the establishment. Unfortunately, it was unlikely that it would be the last.

"I want these two irritants removed from the place. You know how I know important people, Valeria," Cotta issued, flustered, with more than a hint of a threat. He then glared at Varro, not without scorn or a sense of triumph.

The spy smiled in reply, not without a sense of amusement.

"I may know more important people," Varro calmly replied, before reaching into the leather pouch attached to his belt and removing a document. Cotta's eyes narrowed in suspicion as Valeria's aspect widened. The document informed the reader that they should provide any and all assistance to the bearer. It was signed and accompanied by the seal of Marcus Agrippa. The hostess had seen a similar letter before. An agent from Rome had once used the brothel to trap a fugitive one evening.

"I think it best if you do not pursue this matter - and if you leave now, for your sake," Valeria remarked, not without some pleasure after showing the document to the official.

"Now be on your way, you insolent dog," Varro said, goadingly. A few jeers in the background echoed the sentiments.

The humiliated official's face was now flush with anger, as opposed to embarrassment, as he moved towards Varro, letting out a strange gargling noise. The spy was not surprised by the would-be attack. He was a past master at knowing when a victim of his humour would lose his temper. Varro put out his left hand and grabbed Cotta by his tunic. With his right hand he swiftly put the knife, which he had been given to cut his pork chop, to his assailant's throat.

"You can either fight and be filleted like the red mullet on the menu, or head home with your tail between your legs," Varro said, without animus. It was a promise rather than a threat.

The bodyguard standing behind and to the left of Cotta launched himself forward, after seeing the stranger manhandle his master, but he was soon doubled-over and winded from Felix burying his fist in the man's stomach. Valeria's attendants restrained the remaining bodyguard, but he seemed to show no indication of wishing to enter the fray. What with having to work for the odious administrator, he likely wanted to see Cotta come to harm more than anyone else.

"Do let me know if he causes any trouble for you after today," Varro remarked, loud enough for the minor official to hear as he was unceremoniously ushered out of the establishment. "I would dearly love to make his life a misery."

The tension soon dissipated, like storm clouds, and customers went back to staring into their winecups - or at the cleavage on show.

"I am terribly sorry for the disturbance gentlemen. Is there anything I can get you on the house? Anything at all," the hostess said, with a suggestion of suggestiveness.

"I am happy to pay, but I could use an empty but comfortable bed for the night. I suspect that my friend may have a somewhat different request, however," Varro drily remarked, taking in the enamoured, delighted, soppy expression on Felix's countenance as he stared at Fulvia. The life of a spy was preferable to that of a soldier, the young man thought to himself.

***

Felix still possessed a less than martial expression the following morning, as he dwelled upon the previous evening. It would be another long day's ride. The horizon rippled with heat. Varro wished he'd brought one of his sunhats (he purchased them from the same supplier which furnished the Emperor with his). Augustus was known for his fair complexion and keeping out of the sun. He was also known for keeping out of his wife's bed. Not that he was averse to sleeping with a wife - he just preferred it to be someone else's.

Varro's thoughts soon turned again to the events at hand. They would reach the merchant's vineyard by nightfall. The spy recalled his meeting with his spymaster and some of Agrippa's comments concerning Gaius Vettius.

"Vettius inherited his business from his father, who was wise enough to support our side during the civil war - even though Mark Antony and his court of bacchants would have ordered more wine than us. Vettius will cooperate. Merchants are loyal to their treasuries, although I imagine he will wring his hands and profess his loyalty to Rome and the Emperor too. I am not against rewarding our informant for his loyalty, after he has provided you with Dio's location. I will leave it to your judgement, Rufus, in relation to how much you should pay him. You have my permission to be sufficiently intimidating that he will betray Dio for gratis. If you suggest that he contact me. Hint that he could become a favoured supplier for the imperial household. He will doubtless then rub his hands together rather than wring them… It could well prove possible that Vettius will be in the process of fulfilling an order for Dio. You are not beyond the wit of using this to your advantage."

Varro had indeed thought of the seed of an idea. Time would tell whether it would come to fruition. Some wines can mature with age, whilst some can grow sour, he idly pondered as the sun continued to beat down like a small fist.

***

Felix's smile finally disappeared, his posture stiffened. Alert. They had arrived. Through a haze of dust, which had been kicked up from a cart in front, the vines ran straight, like neat script across a wax tablet, for as far as the eye could see. Slaves worked industriously away (though some seem to be wilting in the heat). The villa had a faded grandeur about it (Gaius' father had obtained the property through putting an early bid in, when its previous owner decided to sell rather than have the estate appropriated by the imperial treasury). Coin is more portable than marble - and the republican needed to sail for distant shores.

"What would you like me to do?" Felix asked, as they approached the front of the house.

"Just appear wonderfully intimidating. Look slightly scornfully at Vettius, as though you could easily run him through should I give the order to do so. Most people do more things out of fear than love, unfortunately. Or understandably."

***

Varro instructed the nearest slave to feed and water their horses when they dismounted. Milo. a haughty attendant - with a pointed chin, knitted brow and beak of a nose - strode out of the front door to meet with their unexpected guests. Milo was displeased that someone was intending to try and speak with his master, without arranging an appointment beforehand. His haughtiness soon vanished, to be replaced by due deference and humility, when Varro introduced himself and presented the document from Marcus Agrippa. General. Statesman. Builder of Rome. Right hand to the Emperor himself.

Milo ushered his esteemed guest inside, half ignoring the man's less well attired companion. Although Vettius was probably one of the wealthiest figures in the neighbourhood, Varro's patrician sensibility was unimpressed by the wine merchant's taste and the property's lack of genuine splendour. He did enjoy the smell of grapes and wine which wafted through the villa, though.

Varro sighed with almost as much pleasure as Felix had done the previous night as he took the weight off his feet and sat upon the sofa in the triclinium. The spy noted the cracked mosaic beneath his feet. The merchant probably liked making money, as opposed to spending it. There was an absence of a woman's touch throughout the house. Their host was unmarried, perhaps because of his preference for accumulating wealth rather than haemorrhaging it.

Milo disappeared, his sandals flapping upon the tiled floor as he half ran. The attendant soon reappeared, accompanied by his master, who half bowed whilst wringing his hands as he introduced himself to Marcus Agrippa's representative. Gaius Vettius was middle-aged, and his figure bespoke of a man who lived well. It was far from the most expensive tunic that Varro had ever seen, but far from the cheapest too. The merchant was sharp faced. He had been mistaken for being Gaulish on more than one occasion - and others had spoken of his gall in relation to the prices he charged for certain vintages. Despite his wealth, Vettius often claimed to be struggling - that his margins were as slim as a sylph. "I cannot remember the last time I made a notable profit," he had complained to a client the previous month. "But there are other rewards, like a satisfied customer." Gaius Vettius was as eagle-eyed as a quartermaster when it came to controlling costs. More than women, more than his own produce, the merchant prized efficiency. He was happy to provide credit, but at a cost. He was happy to sell swill to gladiator schools and the finest wines to the finest families in Rome. Making the sale. Making money. It made life worthwhile. Profit and purpose were entwined, like lovers. There were Romans who expressed admiration for either Caesar or Cato. Vettius preferred Crassus. But the wealth which Vettius had accumulated had generated a germ of paranoia. Trust was a commodity in short supply. The merchant felt more fear than distrust, however, after his surprise guest showed him the letter of authority from Marcus Agrippa.

"Please, let me offer you some hospitality. Milo, tell cook to prepare some cooked meats and cheeses from my personal stores. If you also fetch some of our finest Falernian from the cellar. Now, how can I be of service?" Vettius asked, appearing more ashen than usual.

"You supply wine to Publius Dio do you not?" Varro was business-like in his tone. The usual playfulness in his voice was absent.

"I -," Vettius replied, with a catch in his throat.

"I need you to provide his current location to me."

Vettius here experienced a moment of light-headedness, as if he were already a few winecups in. The name immediately flooded his being with dread. Dio was a valued customer and had always acted politely and professionally towards his wine supplier when they met. But Vettius was all too aware of Dio's reputation. The smuggler and moneylender would not forgive any act of treachery. But Vettius was mindful what could happen if he did not cooperate with Marcus Agrippa's agent. The merchant could be taxed into penury and have his assets appropriated in the time it took for Agrippa to sign his name. Cicero could come back from the dead and act as his advocate, but his words would fall on deaf ears.

"Can I ask why you wish to find him?"

"No. I have come here for answers, not questions. You need not concern yourself with matters of the state. Now, do you know Dio's whereabouts? As you can see from the document I handed to you, the penalty will be severe if you fail to cooperate," Varro remarked, his manner uncharacteristically severe. But the role of a spy meant playing a variety of roles.

"I will cooperate, be of service. I know his location. He is only a day's ride from here, near Florentia. I will even furnish you with a map. He should still be there as we are due to make a delivery to him tomorrow. My men are preparing the consignment meant for Dio and his men now."

"Show me," Varro ordered, abruptly, whilst experiencing a groundswell of hope inside. For the first time, the hunter scented of his prey.

***

It was important that the horses were watered, fed and rested. But Varro had no intention of tarrying too long at the wine merchant's estate. He took his time when inspecting Dio's consignment of wine, however. The delivery mostly consisted of acetum, meant for his retinue of bodyguards. But Varro also noted several amphorae for Dio's personal consumption, including a rare vintage that his former drinking companion was particularly partial too. The spy used a small knife to cut open the wax seal and poured himself a measure of the coveted wine. He would duly reseal the container and allow Dio to finish it off.

Vettius remained understandably anxious in the company of Agrippa's agents. He rocked back and forth on his feet and bit his bottom lip, as he watched the spy's young bodyguard wolf down some soft cheeses and his best salted pork. Varro felt a slice of sympathy for the worried merchant and reassured him that, no matter what, Dio would not find out that Vettius was the source of any intelligence. "Should the gods be willing, no one will need fear the smuggler within a day or two." Vettius was not so sure. Dio had disappeared before, he could do so again. He had been known to don disguises, build escape routes into his properties and employ proxies to impersonate him to avoid the authorities and his rivals. To further placate his host Varro put in a significant order of wine to be delivered to his house in Rome. Should he come through his mission unscathed he would want a drink or two to celebrate. He had much to tell Manius. The Briton would happily help make inroads into the consignment when his friend returned to the capital.

Gaius Vettius watched his visitors disappear over the horizon, just to be sure they had left. Although he was obliged to offer them a bed for the evening Varro was happy to stay the night at a nearby tavern. The two fatigued Romans shared a tolerable meal and jug of wine, before sleeping through the night.

They set off at first light for the army camp, situated on the outskirts of Florentia. It was half a day's ride or so. Felix was keen to chat - and he again asked if they would be able to travel back to Rome via *The Sacred Hart* - but Varro largely kept his own counsel. He appeared either deep in thought or sorrow. Vettius was right to worry about any reprisals from Dio, should he slip through the net again. Vettius was aware too that that, like Agrippa, Dio possessed a network of agents. Agents who would not balk at murdering their paymaster's enemies in their sleep, slitting the throats of children and torturing wives in front of husbands. Varro would not be safe in the capital. Nor would Fronto and Lucilla. He regretted not arranging for Agrippa to put them into hiding, until his mission was complete. Dio would be baying for his blood, and the blood of any loved ones. He lamented how his old friend - who he had drank with, shared mistresses with, composed poetry with - had become a monster.

Varro recalled one of the last times he had met his friend, before disappearing out of his life for several years. They had been getting drunk, about to go a-whoring in the Subura. Dio had been discussing how he needed to make his way in the world.

"You have been born into wealth and privilege, my friend. Your life will be a bed of roses, filled with various blooms sleeping next to you," the son of a shopkeeper remarked.

"Would you like me to turn my back on such privilege? I could give my money away to some lepers or leader of one of the new cults springing up in the capital, promising to save the world. Will my misery then make you happy?"

"No, don't be an arse. I just need you to appreciate how I can no longer live a life of leisure like you, or at least not yet. I need to make some money as well as make merry…"

Dio went on to explain how he knew a man, Porcius, a smuggler and moneylender. He had known Porcius for a couple of years and trusted him, "as much as one can trust a rogue." The smuggler had invited Dio to join him and invest in one of his enterprises. Porcius would serve as his mentor, so he could eventually go into business for himself. Varro promised to lend his friend the requisite seed money. Publius soon paid his friend back, with interest. It was the last time they saw one another for some years.

"I do not wish to be in anyone's debt, although I quite like the idea of people being in debt to me," the moneylender confessed.

Varro wondered if - with him furnishing Dio with his initial investment - had he helped create a monster? No matter what the answer to that question was, Varro knew that he now needed to slay the monster.

***

Various soldiers eyed the two strangers with indifference, mild curiosity and a hint of disdain as they advanced towards the fort. Varro remembered how he had visited many a similar camp as a boy, accompanying his father whose job it had been to inspect such facilities - to go through their accounts, assess morale and ensure the soldiers were battle ready. Initially he had been intimidated by the rough-mannered legionaries, but he soon grew to appreciate their bawdy, black humour and admired their sense of duty. They kept Rome safe. No Hannibal would land on their shores anymore. Augustus had secured an enduring peace, partly through defeating an exhaustive list of enemies. Occasionally the soldiers at the fort would be despatched to hunt down bandits. Boredom was perhaps their greatest enemy now. Wine would be the usual weapon of choice, no doubt, to combat boredom. They would play dice and the local brothel would never be short of visitors as well.

Varro showed his document to the officer at the gate. The centurion stiffened to attention. The representative from the capital wished to see the commanding officer. Varro took in the faint smells of ordure, campfire smoke, sweat and garum which pervaded the scene. Bouts of laughter and curse words coloured the air too - and Varro heard part of a ribald joke about a goat, an augur and a one-legged, savage Briton.

Felix reverted to type and gave himself a soldierly bearing, to convey to his fellow soldiers that he was one of them. Yet, in being an agent of the state, he felt a certain pride at being set apart or even above his comrades in rank and importance.

SPIES OF ROME: BLOOD & POISON

The camp commander, one Aulus Curio, strode out of a wooden hut, having just strapped on his sword and brushed crumbs of bread from his tunic. The officer had just been reviewing the accounts from his quartermaster. It was a dull but needful task. Curio did and didn't want to be disturbed. The commander stood taller than most men and, despite being ten years older than the soldiers around him, he was in better condition than them. Muscular. Broken-nosed. Leather-skinned. Stony-faced. Like most commanding officers, Curio appeared serious-looking (bordering on severe-looking). His hair was cropped short. There was a small chunk missing from his right earlobe and Varro nearly winced when he saw a gruesome serpentine scar run along the length of the inside of his left arm. The son of a tanner had been a soldier since late adolescence. He had fought on more than one frontier of the Empire. Aulus Curio believed in the civilising force of Rome, the guiding lights of its laws and superior culture. Rome was a tide of progress, albeit that tide could often prove blood-red. Curio had lost comrades, even a brother, to the cause. He told himself that their sacrifice should not be in vain. The soldier also believed in vengeance - and vanquishing the enemies of Rome, foreign and domestic. The army had brought both purpose and prosperity to his life. He had earned his rank (the same could not be said for some other officers he had encountered over the years, especially the ones who were the sons of prominent politicians).

"You have been sent by Marcus Agrippa, I understand?" Curio remarked, in a stentorian voice. "Do you mind if I see the document?"

"Not at all," Varro replied, handing the letter of authority over.

"I once had the privilege of meeting the Agrippa. He is a great man."

Aye, great at putting me in danger, Varro thought.

The officer's eyes narrowed in either suspicion or scrutiny as he unfurled the scroll. Varro also fancied that he may have taken his time due to being unfamiliar with his letters.

Curio paused, as he stared at the spy like he was on the cusp of ordering his death at any moment.

"How can I help?" the soldier finally stated, his features, as gnarled as a fist, softening slightly. Ever so slightly.

***

Varro was invited into the commanding officer's private quarters, whilst Felix tended to the horses. A fire hummed in the background as the two men sat across from one another, a jug of wine and slab of an unnamed meat between them, as well as a bowl of radishes and honey-glazed carrots. Varro couldn't help but note the array of strange weaponry which adorned one wall - curved blades, leaf-shaped shields, ceremonial spears. Trophies won in battle.

Curio listened intently as the agent explained his mission, occasionally asking the odd question or offering up a comment.

"I know of this man you speak of at this location. I have even met him. He goes under the name of Marcus Rullus. He has visited the camp and generously given wine and livestock to the men around feast days. I always thought there was something amiss about him. The villa Dio occupies is easily defendable, even designed to be defendable. Without the aid of surprise or subterfuge it may prove a tough nut to crack. But crack it we will. I will be able to furnish you with a force of a hundred men, veterans rather than raw recruits, as well as a contingent of archers. We will certainly possess a force which will outnumber our opponent. We just need to make sure we outfox him too. I will accompany you and lead any assault. Hopefully I'll even get to run this cur of smuggler through myself... So, this Publius Dio, who seems as poisonous as this Nightshade you speak of, is an old friend of yours?"

"I'd prefer to classify him as a new enemy," Varro replied, after finishing the dregs in his cup and giving himself a refill.

"Duty calls, eh?"

"And a sense of self-preservation. The bastard made an attempt on my life once. I'd prefer not to grant him a second opportunity. But we will need to catch him first. Dio has been known to employ doubles. I have little doubt that his house will possess an escape tunnel or two. The smuggler is as devious and resourceful as any spy."

SPIES OF ROME: BLOOD & POISON

"I do not envy the world of spies. As a soldier, I need to know that the man standing next to me will keep his sword and shield raised. The role of a spy seems to be to stab people in the back, friend or foe, and vanish into the shadows. Forgive me, it's no slight against you but most spies I have encountered are about as trustworthy as a politician. They lie, just as easily as they breathe. They usually share the same sexual perversions and love of coin too.," Curio argued, draining his own cup and refilling it as well.

"I agree with you, but I may of course be lying when I say that. But know that I have more reason to run Dio through than you. This is one spy you can trust, at least for the next day or two."

"It may seem like an eternity to trust a spy for one day, but I will do so. I may, of course, be lying when I say that, though," Curio expressed, as the soldier permitted himself a rare, wry smile.

The two men worked their way through the jug of wine. Curio surprised himself by how much he enjoyed the patrician's company. Varro may not have spent much time in his adult life in army camps, but few people had spent more time in the taverns of the Subura than the once - or current - dissolute aristocrat. The soldier let out a booming laugh, towards the end of the evening, when Varro told a joke:

"Have you heard about the blind prostitute? You've got to hand it to her."

"I think it best we turn in for the night. We will need to leave at first light. We could well have a long - and bloody - day tomorrow," Curio remarked, after the laughter stopped.

"Hopefully not," Varro pensively replied, almost to himself, as if he knew something the soldier didn't. It was not altogether uncommon for a spy to conceal the truth.

A dull moon hung overhead, surrounded by stars which would one day rust, if they hadn't already lost some of their lustre. Varro walked to his billet for the night with a reassuring confidence in the officer. Indeed, he was more confident about Curio than he was himself. Varro was a reluctant spy - and an even more reluctant warrior. The Roman's stomach felt knotted - and not just because of the undercooked radishes he had eaten.

He may have scented his prey, but Varro had a whiff of fear about him too. He could smell it on himself, as sure as he could smell the dung in the nearby pens containing livestock. So be it. The trick was not to let others smell it. Spying is acting.

***

The dawn was more blood-red than rose-tipped but Varro thought it was a bad omen to think so. It could have been considered a fine day, if the order of the day wasn't death and butchery. Felix handed his companion his sword as they mounted their horses, whilst the hundred approx. soldiers formed up. The young man had kindly sharpened the blade the night before. He had needed a distraction and the soldier wanted to feel useful. Varro couldn't help but sense how the young legionary was straining at the leash to reach their destination and storm the house. Although the spy was happy for Curio to lead front the front, he did not want the youth to put himself in unnecessary danger. Felix believed it was his duty, however, whether self-appointed or directed by Agrippa, to protect the agent. Despite the balmy morning, Varro felt a chill run down his spine as he experienced a grim presentiment - that the soldier would not return from their mission.

Varro was impressed by the speed and order with which the small army assembled itself. The veterans knew their business. That a rumour had spread, that there was potential booty to profit from after the attack, stirred their enthusiasm even more. Some of the soldiers were also looking forward to bloodying their blades.

In the background Varro could hear a drill master give the new recruits a beasting:

"You can't march for shit, you can't dig for shit. I wish I could go back and un-fuck your mothers so that you were never born… The brothel down the road has fewer cunts on offer," the grizzled veteran announced, as his vine stick swished through the air.

The column soon snaked out of the camp. Aulus Curio, on a handsome black mare, led his force so he could control the pace of the march. He wanted to arrive at their destination in good time, but not exhaust the men by doing do. A baggage train brought up the rear. A rhythmic, jangling noise caught Varro's ear as the mass of men marched onwards. Dusty, tanned, determined faces sat beneath burnished helms.

Felix mentioned to Varro how he wished he would have made an offering to Mars before they left. Varro replied that any offering should have been made to Fortuna. The poet - who had read his fair share of Plato, Aristotle and Cicero - was not one to usually put his faith in the gods but there was not much more than one could do but pray as they advanced towards the enemy.

The day wore on. Curio ensured that his men rested and took on water. The chatter was of the potential spoils to be had after the fighting - and that some would be willing to storm the house first to enrich themselves. Varro had an inkling that Curio had instructed his senior officers to sow the rumour about the booty to be won. When the spy hinted as much the commander offered up another wry smile. His men lacked neither courage nor ambition. Curio had one eye on the latter too, Varro suspected. It would not do the commander's career prospects any harm to impress the Second Man of Rome. On more than one occasion Curio fished for knowledge about how close the agent was to Agrippa - and how valuable Varro's favourable report would be.

Curio's keen eye spotted the dust cloud on the horizon first. They were well beyond the midpoint between the army camp and Dio's villa. The commander kicked his heels into the flanks of his mount and cantered towards the two scouts he had sent ahead to reconnoitre the target. Varro duly followed.

The horses - and men - were streaked with sweat and not a little breathless. The scouts - Scaurus and Cato - appeared similar to Varro, like they might have been related. Willowy. Short, bristly hair. Out of uniform. Glum-looking. But that may have had something to do with the news they were about to deliver. The enemy had already fortified themselves, Scaurus explained. A stream ran along the rear of the property and prevented any assault there. Ditches now ran along the sides of the villa, which had oil poured into them - ready to form walls of fire. Scaurus further reported that Dio possessed at least a dozen bowmen. The smuggler's retinue was made up of former soldiers and gladiators. Seasoned killers, who could give his legionaries more than just a bloody nose.

"Bastard," Curio spat. The soldier's expression was still determined - but infused with ire. It was likely that someone from within his own camp was in the pay of Dio and had informed the enemy of the approaching force. Surprise and subterfuge could no longer serve as their allies.

Varro's stomach churned again, and his face turned as pale as a vestal virgin (albeit when the priapic poet had encountered vestal virgins in the past, he had made them blush). Was it not likely that Dio, aware of the advancing soldiers, had already departed? Was he not now on a fool's errand, marching towards the villa? Dio could well be presently racing towards Rome, intent on finding and murdering Fronto and Lucilla. Dio also had the resources to disappear without a trace and strike from afar. Varro recalled Agrippa's words before setting off, "If Dio escapes, you will forever be looking over your shoulder. He will want to kill you, or worse. Make sure you get the job done."

"What do we do now?" Varro asked Curio.

"We do what we always do. We soldier on."

***

The report from the scouts had been accurate, unfortunately. The palatial villa was as fortified as any army camp. The commander offered up another "Bastard" as he surveyed the scene. The sun-baked field next to the property was scarred and pock-marked from the campfires and remnants of where a phalanx of tents had stood, housing Dio's men. Like many things in life, it was a question of numbers and mathematics. Curio had around a hundred men at his disposal. The enemy were around forty or fifty strong. Military thinking dictated that an offensive force needed three times the number of its opponent to defeat a fortified enemy. The officer further harrumphed when he spotted how the ground just before the front of the property was glistening with oil. The commander was perhaps willing to send two "tortoise" units in for a frontal assault. They could defend themselves against a torrent of missiles. But they could not overcome a wall of fire.

"Hopefully the enemy will be duly intimidated and think about surrendering when we fan ourselves out in front of them in a show of strength," Curio had remarked earlier in the day, but there was little hope in his optimism then - let alone now. It was the enemy who were putting on a display of strength and defiance.

Clouds congregated overhead, like lead tiles slotting together to form a roof. The light was fading, like a widow's veil was falling over the world. The temperature dropped, causing another chill to run down Varro's spine, who stood next to the pensive Roman officer.

But all wasn't quite lost.

"Is that your man Dio, standing in the middle on the balcony?" Curio asked.

The spy narrowed his eyes. Focusing. He then widened them in pleasant surprise. His opponent was indeed still present, which only re-enforced Varro's belief that the smuggler had an escape route. He had perhaps constructed a tunnel, leading beneath the stream at the rear and into the woods - where he would have horses waiting. Dio was standing on the first-floor balcony, like a captain at the prow of his ship, issuing orders and sizing up his enemy.

Varro looked to the left of him to see Felix standing by his side, his hand resting on the pommel of his sword. Ready. Willing. Able. Yet Varro tried to think of a reason to excuse the eager soldier from taking part in any assault. The poet couldn't help but imagine the scene of dozens of bloody corpses strewn before the villa. Resembling giant pin cushions, for arrows. Fires roasting flesh. His young friend deserved better than being a feast for crows and flies.

Curio glanced at his men behind. Apprehension was etched into a fair few countenances. And rightly so. The officer trusted that his legionaries were not lacking in courage, but they trusted their commander in return - that he would not throw their lives away needlessly.

A suitably nervous-looking attendant, suffering from a runny nose, was lowered down from the balcony. Under a flag of truce he approached the Roman commander. His eyes flitted to the left and right - and back again - as he took in the long row of steely soldiers. As much as he constantly wiped his nose with his sleeve, and sweat dripped from his temples, the slave's mouth was bone-dry and he almost croaked when he spoke.

"My master would prefer to avoid any bloodshed today and is offering to discuss a potential settlement. He suggests that you talk to him in front of the house. You will be permitted to bring along two soldiers with you."

Curio agreed to the terms. The commander, accompanied by Varro and two soldiers (who stood either side, ready to raise their scutums to defend against any missiles), advanced towards the villa.

"Do you trust him?" the officer asked, knowing the answer already.

"About as much as I trust a scorpion not to sting me. Nor should he trust us, though," Varro replied, fixing his gaze on his enemy, as he stood grinning on the balcony. He may have had a wine or two. Or was drunk on victory.

"Welcome, gentlemen. I suspected that you may be the agent concerned for my welfare, Rufus, but I wanted to know for sure. I like to look my enemy in the eye, before I ruin him. You will learn how to mourn the loss of loved ones – and just when you think you can grieve no more, I will wring more pain from your heart. Drain you of all your blood. May I ask how you found me?" Dio asked, with equanimity, raising his voice so that it carried down below.

"You can ask, but your odds of receiving an answer may be longer than you think," Varro replied, with equal equanimity.

"Sooner or later, you will be compelled to talk. But let us deal with the here and now. I am happy to discuss the terms of your surrender, commander," Dio half-joked, addressing the unimpressed and unamused soldier. "As you can see, I possess the higher ground, so to speak. You can of course roll the dice and attack, but I dare you will end up with the Dog throw. I imagine that you have survived this long as a commander, because you know when you are beaten. At best you will earn a Pyrrhic victory. It is best that you return home and we both go about our business. As for you, Rufus, this is a declaration of war. Agrippa will regret underestimating me. The Second Man of Rome may be untouchable, but I will consider every agent who serves under him fair game, including yourself. Agrippa should have never tried to interfere in my affairs. Like life, I am a necessary evil. I do not create the market for certain goods and services, I just supply it. I did not concoct Nightshade. I am just an honest salesman. You should know better than to judge me as the villain of the piece. Is Agrippa not the greater criminal and swindler, a man who taxes the poor to construct grand buildings to honour a demi-god?"

With his mouth a little dry from his speech Dio called for an attendant to serve him some wine. Varro recognised the jug. The slave had cut off the wax seal earlier, to let the favoured vintage breathe. He carefully poured a large measure into an ornate, gold goblet. His master took a large mouthful.

"Ah. Do not despise me for being better prepared and provisioned than you, Rufus," Publius Dio added, enjoying the bouquet and taste of the morish beverage. "A superior vintage and making money. The two things I never get bored with. I am almost sorry that things have turned out the way they have, my old friend."

"I'm sorry too. This chapter started and has ended with Nightshade," the spy replied, without enmity.

The poison was famed for being tasteless, odourless and deadly. The measure which Varro had taken from the jug at the wine merchant's estate had been replaced with a vial full of the infamous toxin. More than enough to kill more than one soul.

The smile fell from the smuggler's face, as the winecup slipped out of his hand, his lips twisting in a less pleasant expression. It was difficult to discern whether he was experiencing a paroxysm of pain or disappointment. Publius Dio opened his mouth, gurgling. Leaning against the marble balustrade. Perhaps his intention was to let out a curse, call for an antidote or emetic - or order that his archers cut down the enemy. But no one would ever know. Dio immediately felt light-headed, heavy-lidded and blacked out. By the time the slave, who had poured the wine, could fetch some smelling salts his master had passed over.

"Is this what you poets call irony, or poetic justice?" Curio remarked to the spy.

"I do believe it is," Varro replied, consoled by the fact that it was better that a vial of poison had been drunk, than pools of blood had been spilled.

Curio was quick to offer an amnesty to the remainder of the enemy's men. To sweeten the bitter pill of defeat, and to ensure that the seasoned warriors would disperse peacefully, the commander also distributed some of the coin from Dio's treasury into their purses.

It was a matter of "death or glory" people often commentated, when two combatants met in the arena. Varro had avoided death. But he didn't revel in much of a sense of glory. Killing his old friend had been a necessary evil.

A few crows cawed overhead, perhaps complaining that they had been cheated out of a feast of carrion. The dusk thankfully appeared more rose-tipped than blood-red, Varro mused.

***

The spy assured the commander that the remainder of Dio's wine was drinkable, so his men were free to celebrate. The following morning Varro and Felix commenced to travel back to Rome, via *The Sacred Hart*.

"I am not sure that I have earned such a reward," Felix remarked, still suffering from a lingering disappointment at not being able to draw his sword in the name of Rome.

"Never look a gift horse in the mouth, unless she looks like a horse," Varro joked in reply, as the two men rode side by side. "There will doubtless be plenty of times in the future when, as a soldier, you will deserve some spoils of war but be offered none. So take the win now."

Eventually, with their limbs aching, the two companions returned to the capital, just as night was falling. Fronto woke his master early the next morning. Marcus Agrippa was waiting for him in the triclinium.

"You look like you are hung over," the spymaster exclaimed, but with less censure in his voice than usual.

"If only," Varro replied, after yawning and rubbing his weary eyes. "How did you know that I was back?"

"I do possess that most extensive spy network in the Empire. Fronto also kindly sent me a message."

"I'm just surprised you didn't wake me even earlier."

"I thought you deserved a rest, for once. Thank you for your advanced report. I will duly commend Aulus Curio on your recommendation. And how did young Felix perform?"

You should ask Fulvia, rather than me, Varro thought to himself.

"Admirably. The lad now knows when to keep his head down."

"Excellent. You should justly both feel proud. You have helped to vanquish an enemy of Rome," Agrippa pronounced, unable to conceal his satisfaction. Varro suspected, however, that the Second Man of Rome was even more pleased that an ally of the Empress had been defeated.

The reluctant spy was also pleased that it was all over, although part of him remained ill at ease, as if he was still suffering from the dregs of some poison running through his veins. It was nothing that some time and wine couldn't wash away though.

End Note

Spies of Rome: Blood & Poison should hopefully serve as an introduction to the character and world of Rufus Varro, as well as a fun, bonus story to those who are already fans of the series. One of the reasons for returning to the character was that plenty of readers had been in touch to ask for more stories. I also recently gave an interview where I cited Varro as one of my favourite heroes, or anti-heroes.

This will probably be the last time I write about Rufus Varro. But, similar to a spy, one should never entirely trust an author.

Richard Foreman.

Printed in Great Britain
by Amazon